Acting Edition

I0600514

The Nature of Captivity

by Matthew Paul Olmos

FOR PRODUCTION INQUIRIES

UNITED STATES AND CANADA
info@concordtheatricals.com
1-866-979-0447

UNITED KINGDOM AND EUROPE
licensing@concordtheatricals.co.uk
020-7054-7298

Each title is subject to availability from Concord Theatricals Corp., depending upon country of performance. Please be aware that *THE NATURE OF CAPTIVITY* may not be licensed by Concord Theatricals Corp. in your territory. Professional and amateur producers should contact the nearest Concord Theatricals Corp. office or licensing partner to verify availability.

This work is published by Samuel French, an imprint of Concord Theatricals Corp.

No one shall make any changes in this title(s) for the purpose of production. No part of this book may be reproduced, stored in a retrieval system, scanned, uploaded, or transmitted in any form, by any means, now known or yet to be invented, including mechanical, electronic, digital, photocopying, recording, videotaping, or otherwise, without the prior written permission of the publisher. No one shall share this title(s), or any part of this title(s), through any social media or file hosting websites.

For all inquiries regarding motion picture, television, online/digital and other media rights, please contact Concord Theatricals Corp.

MUSIC AND THIRD-PARTY MATERIALS USE NOTE

Licensees are solely responsible for obtaining formal written permission from copyright owners to use copyrighted music and/or other copyrighted third-party materials (e.g. artworks, logos) in the performance of this play and are strongly cautioned to do so. If no such permission is obtained by the licensee, then the licensee must use only original music and materials that the licensee owns and controls. Licensees are solely responsible and liable for clearances of all third-party copyrighted materials, including without limitation music, and shall indemnify the copyright owners of the play(s) and their licensing agent, Concord Theatricals Corp., against any costs, expenses, losses and liabilities arising from the use of such copyrighted third-party materials by licensees. For music, please contact the appropriate music licensing authority in your territory for the rights to any incidental music.

IMPORTANT BILLING AND CREDIT REQUIREMENTS

If you have obtained performance rights to this title, please refer to your licensing agreement for important billing and credit requirements.

THE NATURE OF CAPTIVITY was first produced in a workshop by Mabou Mines/Suite in New York City on March 22, 2011. The performance was directed by Victor Maog, with sets and costumes by Deb O, movement direction by Jennifer Golonka, lighting by James Clotfelter, and sound by Daniel Kluger. The cast was as follows:

NELLIE/ELEANOR . . . . Sarah Nina Hayon
LULU/LUCY . . . . Chantelle Cherisse Lucier
JUSTUS/JUSTIN . . . . Keith Eric Chappelle
GOOCH/GOON . . . . Juan Francisco Villa

PART I – THE OUTSIDE

"Wherever somebody fightin' for a place to stand
For a decent job or a helpin' hand
Wherever somebody strugglin' to be free
Look in their eyes Ma, you'll see me.'

– Bruce Springsteen,
'The Ghost of Tom Joad"

CHARACTERS

JUSTUS – the alpha
NELLIE – the one that needs protectin'
LULU – the one always out the house
GOOCH – in love with Lulu

SETTING

Place

TIME

Just before progress

(Lights up on a salvaged space, broken doen, leftover, it looks like the last structure standing.)

*(A few sounds from outside, like the stepping on branches, like broken cement crumbling, **NELLIE** sits alert.)*

*(Something makes its way into the space, **NELLIE** tenses, but then releases as **JUSTUS** enters holding a dead chicken)*

NELLIE. You scared the shit outta me.

JUSTUS. It's same sound I always make, Nellie, I dunno what you can't tell the difference.

NELLIE. Ya haffta racket everytime you come back, geez.

JUSTUS. I see you lookin'at this chicken, Nellie, don't you be pretending that you ain't.

NELLIE. I can smell it.

JUSTUS. Yea, an what do you smell?

NELLIE. Mostly what I smell is *you*, Jus. Stink much?

JUSTUS. What's a matter?

NELLIE. Nothin', c'mon get that bird over here an let's get it opened up some.

JUSTUS. Let's do it just outside right there.

NELLIE. I heard the shots, ya know.

JUSTUS. Yea, well *they was loud.*

NELLIE. So?

JUSTUS. What.

NELLIE. Don't mess, Jus, just tell me what.

JUSTUS. Awh, c'mon, Nellie, here I brought home something special that we could have together an you just sittin' there pretending you don't care.

NELLIE. I said to get it over so we can open up.

JUSTUS. And I said let's just step outside a few steps and we'll do exactly that.

NELLIE. And I said what was the shots.

JUSTUS. ...tell ya after we eat.

NELLIE. I dunno how I'm goin' eat a thing if there's gunshots in my mind that ain't been accounted for.

JUSTUS. There's been lots of shots ain't been accounted for, Nellie.

NELLIE. Not when Lulu's still out there, Justus.

JUSTUS. Lu's fine.

NELLIE. You seen her?

JUSTUS. No, but –

NELLIE. Then how you know?

JUSTUS. Cuz I looked for her an nothin'.

NELLIE. The shots, Jus.

> *(beat)*

JUSTUS. They hit the bridge, Nellie.

NELLIE. I weren't askin' about no bridge, Jus, I was askin' about shots.

JUSTUS. Who was holdin' up under*neath* that bridge, Nellie?

NELLIE. Can't you ever just answer me what I ask?

JUSTUS. They gone, Nellie. They bloodied up on that heap now. *(pause)* C'mon, Nellie, now it's alright, you cry if you feel to.

NELLIE. Ain't cryin'. That ain't what I do no more.

JUSTUS. What is it then?

NELLIE. What is it??? Lu was with them at that bridge that's what it is!

JUSTUS. There was only three shots, Nellie; three shots an three of them. An Lu weren't one of 'em.

NELLIE. You went to the heap?

JUSTUS. Where you think I come across this chicken you too stubborn to admit yer salivatin' over

NELLIE. I don't salivate.

JUSTUS. So there I is, at the heap. Checkin' to see if they piled anymore things on top –

NELLIE. You mean, if they was goin' pile Lu on top, don't you.

JUSTUS. You wanna hear my tale or don't you wanna hear my tale? Cuz I can stop tellin' my tale and you can just sit there not knowin' shit.

NELLIE. One uh these days, Jus, yer gonna wanna know something that I got inside my head, yer gonna be salivatin' for it, and you know what?

JUSTUS. No, you tell me what.

NELLIE. I ain't gonna give it to ya.

JUSTUS. So, right there, right in the mess and slop of that ol' heap I come across this sloshing about.

NELLIE. Slosh what?

JUSTUS. Oh, Nellie, I don't even know I can describe it for ya.

NELLIE. Well, what it sound like?

JUSTUS. …like when ya step inta something wet.

NELLIE. What it look like?

JUSTUS. …like…

(**JUSTUS** *makes some sort of fucking gesture.*)

NELLIE. What it scent like?

JUSTUS. …like the nastiest leftover juices you ever seen leftover.

(**JUSTUS** *gags,* **NELLIE** *disgusts.*)

NELLIE. Well, what was the hell was it!?

JUSTUS. It was Gooch, crouched an mountin' some bitch that I would not go inside for warmth. An just as he's squishing into her, Nellie, I could see little squirts of juices sprayin' outta her everytime he pushed it in.

(**NELLIE** *gags.*)

NELLIE. Jus, *what* is the matter with you, why'd you go an tell me a foul story like that for?

JUSTUS. Because, Nellie, I want for you to appreciate just what the situation was when I turned from watchin' Gooch squish squish, to hear this pit pat pit pat...

NELLIE. Pit pat pit pat?

JUSTUS. Right there, peckin' along behind me was...

(*JUSTUS mimes with the chicken.*)

Pit pat pit pat...

NELLIE. Oh, pit pat, heh, I get it now.

JUSTUS. So forget the Gooch and I get goin' towards it. Thinkin' how it'll feel when I get my grips, then –

NELLIE. Then what, what?

JUSTUS. The shots, Nellie. Three of 'em. One then two then three. So I throw myself down –

NELLIE. And chicken?

JUSTUS. What about chicken?

NELLIE. Did chicken get down, did the chicken get scared the shots?

JUSTUS. Well, you know what, I don't know what chicken done.

NELLIE. Musta done something.

JUSTUS. Well, I guess when I could hear there wasn't anymore shots to come I looked back, and yea, chicken was pit pat peckin' just like before.

NELLIE. You think chicken didn't hear?

JUSTUS. (*to chicken*) Hey! Hey! Was you heard the shots or nuh uh? Hello??? (*pause*) Well, what do shots mean to chicken anyways, Nellie.

NELLIE. You think chicken don't know shots?

JUSTUS. Well it don't know they're shots.

NELLIE. How could chicken not know they're shots?

JUSTUS. Same as we didn't know they're shots when we first heard' em.

NELLIE. Yea, but after all that what's happened –

JUSTUS. You have to *learn* shots, Nellie.

NELLIE. How do you know one of those shots wasn't, Lulu? I don't think that you do.

JUSTUS. I waited for them tractor machines to pull up.

NELLIE. Yea, so.

JUSTUS. They put three bodies, Nellie, one, then two, then three. An that's it.

NELLIE. Yea, but you didn't see her, you *don't* know –

JUSTUS. There was nothing else inside that tractor machine, Nellie. If they'd uh kept her, I'd have seen her in the nets with all the other shit they collect. Believe in me, Nellie, Lulu is comin' home.

NELLIE. Maybe she with Gooch, maybe Gooch got right up from that smelly bitch an ran as fast as his legs would allow to make sure that his Lulu was okay.

JUSTUS. Well that is not what Gooch done after them tractors moved off, after they put those bodies.

NELLIE. He helped you with the bodies?

JUSTUS. Nellie. I can't just go atop the heap and start removin' bodies, they'll know we're here.

NELLIE. Oh.

JUSTUS. But even if I had been able, I doubt ol' Gooch woulda been much help.

NELLIE. I don't know why you gotta talk so down on Gooch everyday of his life, what's he ever done to us 'cept love after our Lulu everyday, allday?

JUSTUS. Nellie, I'm gonna give you one educated hint as to what Gooch was doin' so special that he did not run after Lu today: Sniff sniff.

(He touches her nose.)

NELLIE. Hey, what're you touchin' my nose for.

JUSTUS. Because I am trying to get you to use a bit of logic, now what was it Gooch was doin' at the beginning of the story?

NELLIE. So what, Jus.

JUSTUS. So what do you think he went back to doin' at the end of the story?

NELLIE. He…he went back to doin' *that?*

JUSTUS. Well, I'm assuming he hadn't finished.

NELLIE. Finish?

JUSTUS. Yea, finish.

NELLIE. How could he wanna finish after where there's been blood!?

JUSTUS. Nellie, only somebody who's never finished could ever ask the question, how could he wanna finish.

NELLIE. Well I'm sorry, but if there are bodies up above, bodies that used to…used to be alive with us –

JUSTUS. Well, doin' that helps.

NELLIE. Oh, you are a nasty, Jus. And that is why you'll never get a family of yer own, you've a rancid mind.

JUSTUS. There ain't a thing wrong doin' that, Nellie. Something you'd know if you ever went outside.

NELLIE. I don't wanna know, Jus, it sounds just about awful.

JUSTUS. Oh, it ain't awful, Nellie.

NELLIE. Oh yes it is, why it uncaring and selfish and apparently it smells awful.

JUSTUS. Smelling awful is part uh what makes it good tho'.

NELLIE. Well excuse me but smellin' awful is not part of what I call good, Jus.

JUSTUS. When yer there, you get a good foothold, an ya just…

NELLIE. Just what?

JUSTUS. You just let go, Nellie. Of everything. Why I used to take my Rose Marie an I'd get that downright slamming, that straight up banging goin' on her! Why, it knocked the worry clean outta her. And me.

NELLIE. Well…I'd like not to worry so much about things.

JUSTUS. An yea, my Rose Marie could smell something godawful sometimes, but smellin' her, tastin' her, scratchin' at her, just bitin' into her and hearin' her

howl through me, Nellie…it's like there we are usin'
all our senses like all at once.

NELLIE. That sounds okay, I guess. But –

JUSTUS. What.

NELLIE. Whys it gotta be so…

(NELLIE *gives a fucking gesture.*)

JUSTUS. Oh, believe you me, Nellie, that is not what you'll
be complaining about when it happens for you.

NELLIE. Whys it gotta be so slamming and banging into.

JUSTUS. Just trust, Nellie, when you are layin' there getting'
thumped nice an solid, you will be wishin' there was
more slamming, more banging into.

NELLIE. An there's another thing, why's it gotta be *me?*
Don't I ever get to give it to them?

JUSTUS. I'm sure they wouldn't mind.

NELLIE. Somebody who's sweet on me, who says the most
kindest things on me, who'll let me give it to them
ever so soft, ever so nice.

JUSTUS. You ever wanna meet anybody you can give it to
like that, Nellie, you're gonna haffta put yerself out
there.

NELLIE. I'll meet somebody, Jus, and I'll go outside to do
it. But not today tho, not with gunshots.

(beat)

Now, c'mon, we better get ready this chicken 'fore Lu
get home.

JUSTUS. Alright, then, split' her into three parts. You sure
you don't wanna just separate it right there in the
door way? I'll be right there with ya. We'll even leave
the door open.

NELLIE. Justus.

JUSTUS. Small steps, Nellie, if you don't take them, ain't
nothin'gonna ever change.

NELLIE. …just I think what if the feathers fly off and give
us away that we're here.

JUSTUS. You know they're gonna find us, Nellie.

NELLIE. You don't know that, Justus, I know that you don't.

JUSTUS. Nellie.

NELLIE. Maybe they'll forget to check this spot. Maybe they'll make some of them new buildings so tall that they'll shadow us, make us easy to overlook.

JUSTUS. No, Nellie. They'll come here. With their strange voices and their loud noises. And if they see us still here livin' –

NELLIE. Ma wouldn't let them.

(*awkward silence*)

JUSTUS. Ma's not in a place to help us anymore, Nellie.

NELLIE. You shut up, Jus; she's strong all places. Ma an Lulu are gonna not let them. Cuz they're females, females who are strong.

JUSTUS. *Lulu* almost got herself killed today! *(beat)* I tried tellin' em, but *no* they all had it in their stupid heads they was just gonna go right up to them strange voices/ tractor machines and welcome them right on in.

NELLIE. But how come if we was friendly to them, how come they...

JUSTUS. Ever since they showed up in that boat thing uh theirs, you seen' em make one act uh niceness to us? No, nuh-uh, they not here ta be welcomed, Nellie. They here cuz they want something an they don't care who or what be in their way.

NELLIE. What *do* they care about then?

JUSTUS. I don't know, Nellie.

NELLIE. Well, just cuz it didn't work talkin' to em at the bridge today, that don't mean it won't ever work –

JUSTUS. They don't talk, Nellie, they DO! *(pause)* You've never seen'one of'em, have you?

NELLIE. They eat don't they? They breathe in an out just like we do. They got hearts, hearts with blood in them, same as we got...

JUSTUS. When this is all over. When this whole distress is done…I'm goin' *cut* one uh them open for you, Nellie. I'm goin' cut one uh them open an show you how their insides aren't nothing like how ours are. Any hearts they have probably are made with sharp an harsh edges, any blood they pump is likely thick and ugly-colored like oil, and I'll show you, Nellie, how everything will be twisted and not in the right place. There will be *something* to explain why they do the things they do!

NELLIE. …I don't want you to cut anyone open, Justus. I don't imagine it'll help any. *(beat)* C'mon, why don't we get ready the chicken 'fore Lu get home.

JUSTUS. You wanna do the feathering, so you can make sure none of the feathers fly away?

(NELLIE stops, looks at JUSTUS.)

NELLIE. None of the feathers fly away??? *(pause)* You mean I had a right thought, Justus, what I said about the feathers flying off? You mean I was right about that?

JUSTUS. …yea.

(NELLIE eagerly defeathers the chicken.)

You had a right thought, Nellie, a real right one.

NELLIE. It's nice you know, Jus, when you say stuff like that.

JUSTUS. Stuff like what, Nellie?

NELLIE. Stuff like about how when somebody done right, instead of how always they've done wrong.

(JUSTUS pulls a piece of meat off the chicken and bites in, then offers to NELLIE who pauses.)

Should we really be eatin', we don't even know where Lu at.

(JUSTUS puts a piece of chicken at NELLIE's nose, she cannot resist, she devours a pull of meat. They begin to feed ravenously, lights remain low over them while across the stage, lights pullup on GOOCH, who waits outside; we hear the sounds of nature; insects, birds, wind. LULU enters. He jumps a bit.)

GOOCH. That you, Lu?

LULU. Well, look who it is.

GOOCH. Course it's me, you know I always wait for you.

LULU. What are you looking at me like that for, Gooch?

GOOCH. Are you, hurt or –

LULU. Shot?

GOOCH. Yea, that I guess.

LULU. Do I look shot to you?

GOOCH. No.

LULU. Well, there you go then.

GOOCH. I was so –

LULU. So what?

GOOCH. Worried, worried that you –

LULU. That I?

GOOCH. I guess they didn't take to kindly to your welcoming wagon, huh?

LULU. If you mean they murdered everyone but me, then no, not too kindly.

(**LULU** *begins to laugh,* **GOOCH** *tries to join. Soon actual laughter takes them both over. A few moments.*)

GOOCH. Wait, what're we laughing for, that ain't funny.

LULU. We're not laughing because of funny, Gooch, we're laughing because what else is there. *(pause)* Really, Gooch, what else is there?

GOOCH. Just us, I guess. And Nellie. Justus too.

LULU. Know what I have been thinking about tho', Gooch?

GOOCH. I never know what you're thinking, Lu

LULU. Love.

GOOCH. Love?

LULU. Yea, like loving. Like to love. Like being loved.

GOOCH. I'm listening.

LULU. What do you think, Gooch, about loving a different kind than us? A different sort.

GOOCH. How do ya mean?

LULU. I mean look at us. There isn't anymore of us left. And all the love that used to be between our family, yours, it's gone. So now, we'll have to learn to love other kinds of families.

GOOCH. What other kinds?

LULU. You know what other kinds, Gooch. The only other kinds there are now.

GOOCH. Sometimes I can't sleep, so I think about how warm things could be. To lay next to, to be my face alongside some other face. An it don't even matter, I suppose, what kinda face. Any kind. It don't matter.

LULU. I think if I had to, if I was put somewhere with no other things to love, I might. I might be able to. If I had to, Gooch, I think I could love most anything

GOOCH. 'Cept me, huh?

LULU. Gooch, can I ask you.

GOOCH. Do.

LULU. All these years, all these days, you've known there wasn't any chance I'd ever look across at you the same way you look across at me.

GOOCH. Thank you for reminding me.

LULU. So what do you follow me around then for?

GOOCH. I don't stay by you, Lu, because I think I'll change your mind. But what else can I do? It's either be near you or don't be near you. It's an easy choice.

LULU. And do you know *they* won't ever change their minds out there, Gooch. They didn't come to this place to change their minds about anything.

GOOCH. Okay.

LULU. So we can either stay hiding out till they find us and be put up on that heap or we can –

GOOCH. But you don't know, Lu, you don't how come they put some in the nets and not others; you don't know nothing about why they do.

LULU. I been watching them, Gooch. An I believe it that if we put ourselves over by that one building, the one where they take all the shit they collect, I believe it that they might figure us for a couple of strays that got loose somehow. An take us on inside. Alive.

GOOCH. Yea, but inside what?

LULU. I don't know.

GOOCH. At night, sometimes I can hear' em. Our kind. Inside that building thing. They don't sound too happy.

LULU. Least they still breathing, Gooch.

GOOCH. Least they're all together.

LULU. So what do you choose, Gooch? Its either wait for that heap or –

GOOCH. You know what I choose, Lu.

LULU. Say it.

GOOCH. You. I choose you, Lu. That's what I'll always choose, no matter what the question.

LULU. It's good to see you're taking this seriously, Gooch.

GOOCH. What about Nellie.

LULU. …I couldn't do that to her.

GOOCH. Oh, just to me, huh?

LULU. If Nellie not once has to see any of this with her own eyes –

GOOCH. She an Jus probably worried for you, Lu.

LULU. You don't mention this to either of 'em, Gooch, do you understand me?

GOOCH. I'll never understand you. But okay.

LULU. C'mon then, let's – *(pause)* What is, Gooch? *(pause)* You sure you wanna come with me, Gooch?

GOOCH. …yea. That's the only thing I ever been sure of, Lu.

(They walk. Lights shift to **JUSTUS** *and* **NELLIE** *wiping the grease from their mouths with enjoyment; chicken bones on the floor; time has passed, it is getting dark. A sound heard offstage, both look up.)*

NELLIE. It's Lu!

JUSTUS. Stay you down, Nellie, till you hear me say otherwise.

(**NELLIE** *quickly hides herself away.* **JUSTUS** *opens the opening. Notices something.*)

Hey, not only can I see yer ugly head stickin' out, but I can smell ya just as good. C'mon now 'fore yer stink give us away.

(**GOOCH** *enters.*)

Now what is the point of hidin'like that?

GOOCH. I didn't wanna bother you is all.

NELLIE. That you Gooch?

GOOCH. Yea, Nellie-belly, it's me.

(**NELLIE** *pops up.*)

JUSTUS. Nellie, what did I tell you about stayin' put?

NELLIE. It's just Gooch, what's he ever brought harm to?

JUSTUS. If I say it to you ta stay put, than you do that till I unsay it.

NELLIE. Justus, that don't make no sense –

JUSTUS. Down, Nellie, now.

(**NELLIE** *gets down.*)

GOOCH. Are you just gonna let Nellie stay down like that?

JUSTUS. Are you a part of this family, Gooch?

GOOCH. …no, I suppose I'm not.

(*Enter* **LULU**.)

LULU. Justus. Nellie.

(**JUSTUS** *glares at* **LULU**, *who goes about her business.*)

JUSTUS. *(to* **LULU**) Really???

LULU. What.

JUSTUS. That's all you got to say?

LULU. Oh, sorry. How are you? Nellie, how's it going?

NELLIE. Well I didn't get shot, so…y'know, that's good.

LULU. An Justus?

JUSTUS. No, I wasn't shot either, Lu. Yourself?

LULU. I seem to have avoided that for one more day. Good to be home.

JUSTUS. Yea, *home.* I'm glad you remember that.

LULU. So…wow, did you all hear the shots today?

NELLIE. I did!

GOOCH. I heard 'em too.

LULU. And how about you, Justus, did you hear the shots. There was 1, 2, 3 of 'em.

JUSTUS. I can do you better than that –

NELLIE. He was at the heap today!

JUSTUS. Hey Gooch, what happened to that smelly ol' piece anyways, where'd she run off too?

GOOCH. I don't know.

JUSTUS. Ya don't know?

LULU. You don't even know if she's okay, Gooch, if she's even –

GOOCH. She got a hidin' spot. A real good one

JUSTUS. Good, where is it?

GOOCH. Well, it wouldn't be that good if I went around telling about it.

JUSTUS. Yea, well if they close in on us, maybe we could –

GOOCH. There's no room. It's…it's just room for one, barely that even.

JUSTUS. Oh, well forget that idea then.

(**JUSTUS** *tosses a piece of chicken at* **LULU.**)

Apologies, Gooch, don't mean to tease ya, but, hell, you must be used to that.

NELLIE. What's that supposed ta mean, Jus? Gooch's gotta be hungry, specially after all that thumpin'he been doin'.

GOOCH. Don't you worry about it, Nellie. Justus is right, he's gotta watch out for you and Lu, that's what he's gotta watch out for.

NELLIE. But…if yer hungry, an we got food. It don't make no sense that three of us sit with our bellies okay while one of us not.

JUSTUS. Nellie, we put the chicken into three parts, one for me, you, and Lu. We didn't put it into four.

NELLIE. That's how come Gooch can't eat, cuz numbers?

LULU. Gooch, go on, have a bite, I ain't even all that hungry.

(She tosses to **GOOCH**, **JUSTUS** *aggressively takes it away and forces it back to* **LULU**.*)*

Jus, it's my share, what do you care what I do with it.

JUSTUS. I am not out there everyday puttin' myself right in the middle of danger for just anyone, Lu. I'm doin' it cuz you two is my family, and Ma set me to take care of you.

LULU. Ma wouldn't have had anybody go starving, Justus.

GOOCH. Please, I don't need anything, I'm not –

NELLIE. You had you some good canned food today, huh?

GOOCH. Yea, Nellie, why I found me three or four good cans almost all the way full. You shoulda seen the way I stuffed my Gooch-belly today. See that, lookit how round.

NELLIE. It don't look round.

JUSTUS. If Gooch wanted help in getting food, he shoulda got his own family.

LULU. He had his own family, Jus, an they died. Yers just happened to not. It ain't his fault to be alone.

JUSTUS. Well then he coulda started his own new family then, couldn't ya, Gooch.

GOOCH. Please don't get a raise in voices over me.

LULU. You didn't start any family, Jus. You just lucked into this one.

JUSTUS. If all this hadn't come about, me an Rose Marie'd have us a family right here in this spot. An there I'd have two families. You tellin' me Gooch can't get one?

LULU. Yer no better than he is, Jus, yer just luckier.

JUSTUS. Life don't have luck, Lu. It has effort. And anybody who has anything will tell you same.

LULU. And anybody who don't have anything, what will they tell you?

JUSTUS. They'll tell you that nothing is their fault, that they just stumbled onto some bad luck. And that's how come

LULU. How come what?

JUSTUS. How come everything.

NELLIE. But, Gooch tried, Justus, he tried harder than anybody I ever known. He been tryin' with Lulu since I don't even know cuz I wasn't born yet.

JUSTUS. That ain't tryin', Nellie. That's just stupid.

LULU. Oh, really, Jus and why is that.

GOOCH. You all do realize I'm standing right here, right?

JUSTUS. Because it ain't trying if you got no chance, is it?

NELLIE. Awh, he's got a chance, don't he, Lu?

JUSTUS. Yea, Lu, answer her. Do he?

GOOCH. Still standing. Right here.

LULU. And because he doesn't have a chance with me, Justus, what do you propose he do?

JUSTUS. Something else.

LULU. What else.

JUSTUS. Anything else.

LULU. Give me an example.

JUSTUS. Lu, I don't have the first slightest idea what Gooch ought to have done with his life besides waste it next to you. I have my own life and family to worry over.

GOOCH. Maybe I should go.

LULU. Don't go.

NELLIE. Yea, stay! That way I got somebody to watch them fight with.

LULU. What if, Justus, I was the last female in existence? What if there were no other females, not anywhere. What would you suggest Gooch do then?

JUSTUS. You know, I really am glad with all the shit that is going on right outside our home, you somehow find the time to drag me into these stupid –

LULU. What should he do?

JUSTUS. ...fine, so in this so very realistic scenario, does he have a chance at a family with you or don't he?

LULU. No, he does not.

JUSTUS. With no other choices in life, then yes, I suppose he might as well just follow you around as opposed to bein' –

LULU. What.

JUSTUS. Alone.

LULU. So it's better to settle for almost, than it is to have nothing?

JUSTUS. That's a weird way to sum it up, but okay.

NELLIE. Wait, are we still talking about Gooch and the chicken?

JUSTUS. I doubt it.

LULU. So can he?

JUSTUS. Can he what?

LULU. Have some of my chicken, it is the last piece left

JUSTUS. Yer goin' do what you want anyways, Lu, no matter how much I care. Always have. Matter of fact, it don't even have weight how much somebody love and care for you, do it? Lulu is gonna do what's best for Lulu, everytime.

LULU. Least I don't let hungry go hungry.

(**LULU** *gives piece to* **GOOCH**, *who devours it.*)

NELLIE. Thought you was full up, Gooch?

GOOCH. Maybe them canned foods wasn't as full as I thought, Nellie-belly.

JUSTUS. So?

LULU. What.

JUSTUS. What, did we just meet, like for the first time, is that what you think?

LULU. Do you think they're ever gonna stop looking for us, do you?

JUSTUS. Well if we –

LULU. And if/*when* they do find us, do you think there is any chance they're not gonna just shoot us down, then cut our throats.

(**NELLIE** *gasps.*)

JUSTUS. Lovely.

Nellie, you can thank your sister for how you sleep tonight.

NELLIE. Is that what...how come they cutting our throats for??? Why would they...cut our throats for?

GOOCH. Oh, they don't cut *all* the throats, Nellie-belly. Just...you know...most of 'em

JUSTUS. An now you can thank Gooch for you sleep tomorrow night.

NELLIE. What do they do when they *don't* cut the throat?

GOOCH. Well –

LULU. Gooch.

GOOCH. Some of 'em they don't cut nothing. They shoot you in the leg, sure –

JUSTUS. Well, this is *much* better.

GOOCH. They have to keep you from running, but then –

LULU. GOOCH.

GOOCH. *Without* hurting, they take you up into a net thing and carry you back to one of their buildings where they let you live for ever and ever.

NELLIE. And ever?

GOOCH. Uh huh, Nellie, just like that.

NELLIE. Well who the heck would want the cut throat thing, let's go do the ever and ever option!

(JUSTUS *glares at* GOOCH.)

JUSTUS. No, go on, Gooch, I'm curious myself how yer gonna back yer way outta this one.

LULU. Maybe he doesn't have to.

(JUSTUS *looks at* LULU, *then grabs her, forcing her outside. Split scene, as* GOOCH *and* NELLIE *stay inside awkwardly.*)

NELLIE. That means they want to "have a discussion that I wouldn't be able to contribute to."

GOOCH. It's probably best that way, Nellie.

NELLIE. But I meant what I said, if living forever and ever is something we can do, why don't we just do that?

(outside)

JUSTUS. Where you been all day?

LULU. You got something to ask, Jus, ask it.

JUSTUS. Were you over by those buildings? Were you?

LULU. No, Jus, I promise to you, I was not.

JUSTUS. If you think for even a second I'd let Nellie be put into one uh them buildings –

LULU. I wouldn't either, Jus, of course not.

JUSTUS. Well, I know Gooch didn't just come up with that scenario all on his own.

LULU. No, neither would I.

JUSTUS. So…?

LULU. I want for Nellie exactly what we discussed; the less she see, the better

JUSTUS. I'd rather have my throat cut a thousand times than her see just one time what me an you seen.

LULU. Gooch wasn't supposed to speak.

JUSTUS. About what.

LULU. What you agreed with, Justus. We don't have any other choices. We are down to just those two. And I'd rather settle alive than dead

JUSTUS. We said ta Ma we would not separate. Not ever.

LULU. That was a different world, Jus.

JUSTUS. You, me, and Nellie is the only world there is.

LULU. No, it's not. And maybe if that wasn't how you think, we might –

JUSTUS. Might, what!?

LULU. Don't get me wrong, Jus, I appreciate what you done for us. I do. But…

JUSTUS. Say it!

LULU. Maybe if you hadn't told every family to watch for their own an that's it, maybe we could have helped each other, we could have come together, we could've –

JUSTUS. *That* is how we get by, Lu, that's exactly how Ma got by too. You think she worked herself like she done that for anybody but us three?!

LULU. No, Justus, maybe you don't remember or maybe you don't want to remember, but when we were young, you couldn't tell any of us apart. There'd be so many little ones running around from house to house, and everyone's door was open. There was no this-is-ours an that-is-theirs. It was all everyone's And it was you, after she got weak, it was you that started telling us to mark what was ours and keep what we had to our own.

JUSTUS. Our mother was not going to be here anymore, Lu, we had to prepare, we had to make sure we had enough for Nellie to –

LULU. Nellie would've had hundreds of enough, she would've been surrounded by it! But instead, she just had you and me. The three of us behind closed doors.

JUSTUS. It wasn't safe anymore.

LULU. It wasn't safe because everyone sitting alone by their separated selves getting picked off one by one. Of course they weren't safe, because for all your protection, Justus, for all your posturing about, all you really did was make everyone by themselves. What do you think your Rose Marie run off for, *if* she run off.

JUSTUS. She's alive, Lu. She's off somewhere safe, I know it that she is.

LULU. Believe what you want, but we are alone here. Even with each other, we are the last ones left. And we have no more choices left ta make.

(inside)

GOOCH. And you see that's how possibilities work, Nellie-belly.

NELLIE. I see.

GOOCH. The number say while it may be possible that you'd live forever and ever –

NELLIE. And ever, yea.

GOOCH. More than likely –

NELLIE. I'd be shot in the leg, then have my throat cut across with blood all over, before they dump me onto the heap.

GOOCH. Precisely.

NELLIE. I admit I don't know much about it, but I'm beginning to think I hate numbers.

GOOCH. Me too.

NELLIE. And while I like talking to you an all, Gooch, I don't really. I'm gonna see what Lu and Jus are discussing through.

(Enter JUSTUS and LULU. Awkward silence.)

GOOCH. So...I'm wondering, as its dark outside an all, if it might be possible I might stay here tonight?

JUSTUS. What for, you been outside in the dark before.

GOOCH. Well, I mean, I guess cuz...everyone else got killed today, that's the main reason, if I had ta pick.

JUSTUS. Don't you stay with that piece from the heap sometime, isn't that what you do?

GOOCH. ...oh, you're right. I'm an idiot. I'll just stay with her, I guess. Well. G'night to you, Nellie-belly, a –

(LULU shoots JUSTUS a look.)

JUSTUS. Do you snore?

GOOCH. Yea.

NELLIE. Oh, you goin sleep by Lulu?! That's so nice. See, Jus, not everything got to be so harsh, just the two of 'em layin' nice by each other. An there's nothin' nasty about it.

JUSTUS. Well, look, just layin' near Lulu ain't gonna keep you warm, 'specially considering how cold she been to you for…your entire life. You goin' have to go out an scrounge up yer own things to keep warm with, lay on top of.

GOOCH. Is that okay, Lu?

LULU. You don't need to go get yer own anything, Gooch, we got enough right here.

JUSTUS. Oh, no we do not. I had to take some of the shit with our scent an put 'em way over past the water to throw 'em off where we at.

LULU. Fine, but Gooch, when yer out there, scrounging up, you feel free to bring back whatever you see fit for any of us. There ain't no reason for you to go an put yourself in danger just for yourself. From here on out, there is no more this is for you an that's for me. We're together.

GOOCH. Alright, I'll just be…

(GOOCH *moves to exit, nobody pays attention. He exits.*)

JUSTUS. Yer just givin' him more work, you realize. You put that in his head, he's goin' be out there for three times as long.

NELLIE. You bringing up a lotta numbers today, Jus.

JUSTUS. Nellie, if you don't shut yer mouth, I'm gonna take away a couple of them pillows you like so much an see if you don't stay up half the night tryin' to count how many you got left.

NELLIE. I stay up the whole night anyways, Jus, I dunno what you go thinking half.

JUSTUS. Wha's that mean?

NELLIE. It was numerical, Justus, you oughta understood it real real good

JUSTUS. You ain't sleeping?

LULU. Nobody is.

JUSTUS. Why not.

NELLIE. What was you an Lu discussin' outside?

JUSTUS. Nothing.

NELLIE. Fine, then I don't know why I ain't sleeping. It's a complete fuckin' mystery.

LULU. Its okay, Nellie, let's just nevermind all that, okay.

JUSTUS. Yea, let's just nevermind everything. We'll nevermind what we have each other, we'll nevermind the whole world and just settle, ain't that right.

LULU. Its okay if yer not sleeping, Nellie, pretty soon all that not sleeping'll add up and then guess what.

NELLIE. What?

LULU. Poof, without even noticing, your eyes will shut, and they'll stay shut for a long time, until you aren't sleepy anymore.

NELLIE. And then what?

LULU. Then when you wake up, you won't feel the awful that you do now.

NELLIE. Is that what you an Jus was discussin' out there then, the future uh my sleep patterns?

JUSTUS. The moment you two go over there, Lu. We're done. They'll never let you back out again. We'll just begin breeding and rebreeding underneath them. An that'll be who we are.

LULU. Least I'll be able to sleep.

JUSTUS. Will you, Lu? Or will you always be on alert. The smallest sound, the most distant notice and your whole body will jump up scared. Cuz you'll be in their world, not ours. And no matter how long you stay there, they'll never let you forget that.

NELLIE. Jus, what're you talkin' about, I don't like it, what're you talkin' about.

LULU. Nothing, Nellie. He's just, he just wants us all to sleep better that's all.

NELLIE. You goin' somewhere, Lu. You an Gooch?

LULU. Of course not. Gooch is out gettin' us all stuff. Huh, won't that be nice, Nellie, having one, two, three, four of us in here, just like how it used to be.

NELLIE. I wanna know what you two was yellin' at outside.

JUSTUS. Nellie, I'm sorry. That was my fault. I told her not to go the bridge today, but she went anyways. And well, we know how that turned out. I was just telling her how I told her so. How I wish she'd listen to me, how close she got to bein' hurt, how lucky she was, that once.

LULU. C'mon, Nellie, why don't we lay you down.

NELLIE. I'm not stupid, you know.

LULU. Never stupid, Nellie.

JUSTUS. Just a few years younger is all.

NELLIE. Don't talk numbers to me, Jus! Not once more.

LULU. Sleep, Nellie.

JUSTUS. Listen to yer sister.

NELLIE. Know how come I'm not stupid?

JUSTUS & LULU. Why.

NELLIE. Cuz you two never agree on anything. The only time you two bandy up is when yer lying to me.

LULU. We'll talk about it in the morning.

JUSTUS. We'll talk about it in the *afternoon.*

NELLIE. Why the afternoon?

JUSTUS. No reason, Nellie, I was just trying to disagree with Lu, so you'd feel more at home.

NELLIE. …is it…is it cuz in the afternoon Gooch and Lulu will be out by those buildings, trying to get that net put around them? Is that why, is it…

(A silence. NELLIE breaks down.)

LULU. Nellie?

JUSTUS. You okay, Nellie?

LULU. Nellie, c'mon, of course that's not why.

JUSTUS. Breathe, Nellie.

NELLIE. …

LULU. Nellie?

NELLIE. …*(NELLIE weeps.)* …how…how could you go out there, Lu, you don't have to go with them, …there's horrible things out there, …how could anyone…?

*(A single, crystal gunshot is heard from just outside. A bit of commotion, strange voices. Lights focus to **NELLIE**; we are someplace else, somewhere quiet. **NELLIE** savors the quiet, we see more strength in her than we have previously seen.)*

If I was a bullet…I'd be so proud. Always when I hear them go off, even from that very first time…always I imagine. They sit, inside the gun machine. So warm and snug. Other little bullets snug next to them.

*(**NELLIE** acts like a bullet.)*

(to other bullets) Hey. Hi. Warm in here, isn't it?

An I bet you they don't wanna go. In fact, I bet you they would stay inside that gun machine for all their lives, just sitting, like this. *(pause)* But I guess that's not what bullets were invented for. Staying put. *(pause)* They have to go somewhere. Out. Into the world. But know why it'd be okay to be a bullet? Cuz yougettogososofast! *(pause)* So fast they move that I wanna SCREAM! *(pause)* And finally, they're someplace else.

*(**GOOCH** appears close to **NELLIE**, she lands in him. There is blood coming out of his chest. **NELLIE** backs away, scared.)*

But a bullet doesn't know where he or she is going. They just go. Because somebody makes them so. Somebody makes them. So they go. I don't think anyone should be made to go anywhere. You should only go where you want to. Bad stuff happens when forced to go. Bad stuff happens. Like that.

(*NELLIE* watches **GOOCH** *crumple to the floor, wounded.*
NELLIE's *light goes out; her quietness ends.*)

LULU. Omigod, Gooch…

(*All frantically surround* **GOOCH**, *trying to help.*)

JUSTUS. Nellie, get me some water then I need ya ta put
pressure right here. (*pause*) Nellie, go!

(*NELLIE* does.)

Lu, you talk to him, let him hear your voice. (*pause*) Lu!

(**JUSTUS** *digs into the wound*, **NELLIE** *pours water.*)

LULU. Hey there, Gooch, it's me. Lulu. Yea, I'm right here
close. Just like you always wanted. With you an not
goin' no place. Can you hear me?

(**GOOCH** *gets up and joins* **LULU** *downstage, while*
JUSTUS *and* **NELLIE** *still tend to his body on the floor*
upstage.)

GOOCH. Of course, I can hear you, you're talkin' into my
ear, love.

LULU. I shouldn't've sent you out.

GOOCH. You didn't send me, I went.

LULU. I'm sorry, Gooch, sometimes I am *so* sorry.

GOOCH. Just sometimes?

LULU. …how are ya feelin', Gooch?

GOOCH. Well, your brother is trying to dig a bullet out of
my chest. I've felt better.

LULU. How did –

GOOCH. Doesn't matter. They woulda got me soon enough,
I always come by here at night. To make sure you're
okay. To see you're safe

LULU. …I didn't know that.

GOOCH. Every night.

LULU. Who was it that –

GOOCH. They all look alike to me. (*pause*) You don't
though, you look one-of-a-kind. Holding over me. My

God, look at you. If there was anything ever I wanted to be lookin' at while my breathin' stopped…it's you.

LULU. You shouldn't talk like that.

GOOCH. It's true. You're it for me.

LULU. Even when you're at the heap today?

GOOCH. *(smiling)* You shoulda seen the smell.

LULU. I can imagine.

GOOCH. Know something? *(pause)* They all smell like that when they're not you.

(**LULU** *looks back at where his body is; worried.*)

NELLIE. Jus, what's wrong, how come he's shivering like that for?

JUSTUS. Means he's givin' a fight, Nel. I just need ta…if I can just…

(**JUSTUS** *digs further.*)

LULU. You never give up, do you?

GOOCH. If you don't have what you want, what else have you got.

LULU. They're close by then?

GOOCH. Yea, this is about the last spot left.

JUSTUS. Come on!

NELLIE. Easy, Jus, you don't wanna bury it in further.

(**JUSTUS** *slips,* **NELLIE** *has trouble holding* **GOOCH**'s *shaking body down.*)

That's too much blood, too much.

LULU. Hey, lookit me.

(**LULU** *holds* **GOOCH**'s *face.*)

You see me?

GOOCH. Oh yea.

LULU. You can do this. You just keep not' givin' up like how you do with me. You hear me.

JUSTUS. He's lost too much.

NELLIE. No, keep tryin, keep tryin'.

JUSTUS. I…I don't know much else I can do.

GOOCH. I think this is it, Lu. I think that's clear.

LULU. No. You're wrong. You're gonna stay the night here, with me. Just like how you always asked. Layin' right up close. You'll be wrapped around me like…

GOOCH. You don't have to –

LULU. Shut up. Wrapped around me like…

GOOCH. Like death, Lu?

> (**LULU** *kisses* **GOOCH**. *Meanwhile* **JUSTUS** *stands back up, he and* **NELLIE** *looking sorrowfully down at the body.*)

JUSTUS. I can't do nothin' more

NELLIE. But…

JUSTUS. Was too deep.

NELLIE. Is he…oh god, is he…

JUSTUS. Yea. He is, Nellie.

> (**LULU** *and* **GOOCH** *finish their kiss.* **GOOCH** *looks back at his now lifeless body.*)

GOOCH. I got to go.

LULU. No, please. Just…

GOOCH. C'mon, Lu, don't make my last sight be you cryin'.

LULU. I'm sorry all the time for how I was. I'm sorry I wasn't nicer.

GOOCH. Hey, you were honest. And you're here now.

LULU. But –

GOOCH. Hey Lu.

LULU. What?

GOOCH. I'm happy. Right at the end…I am. Cuz of you.

LULU. I'm goin' miss you, Gooch. I will. I do.

GOOCH. Know what? I believe you.

> (**GOOCH** *memorizes her neck, then returns to his body.*)

JUSTUS. Know what he'd say if he could still speak? *(pause)* "On my last day, I got to give it good an hard to some nameless piece in the morning, and by night I was bein' kissed by the one I love and always will." That's a pretty good day.

NELLIE. Least he never was up on that heap, least he had that.

JUSTUS. They ain't gonna get no more bodies on that heap. They've had their last.

LULU. I don't know if I'm cryin' over him, like who he was...or that I'll never be loved as I was again...

JUSTUS. It's good that you are, Lu, cryin'. He'd appreciate.

NELLIE. How come they gunshot him for though, what'd he do?

JUSTUS. He was here. That's all it takes.

LULU. They'll be here soon. They will.

(A beat. Lights close-in on **NELLIE**.*)*

NELLIE. I know I said earlier how I'd wanna be a bullet but...honest, I don't really understand the gun machine.

Like why it was invented for.

Like I've never even seen one. Just only heard how loud. *(pause)*

I imagine the gun machine to be very, very heavy.

And if I were to touch it...it'd be so hot, probably burn my...

(illustrates her hand)

It's got metal, I know that much. I understand it's fast, like I was saying. And it does that...

(illustrates **GOOCH***'s body)*

...that much I know real good.

I guess I don't understand what they need them for. I mean I get it that they need them to put the bullets go realreal fast. But...why do they even wanna do that?

Why did they bring them along on that boat thing when they got here? What were they expecting to find that they'd need mean things like that for? And *before* they got here, what did they do with them? Did they make the gun machines go loud on each other, on their own kind?

I got so many questions I'd like to know the answers to, but…maybe I'm better off, maybe I haven't got the mind to understand anyways. And maybe, oh this might sound awful to say, but maybe I wish their boat thing had sunk down into the cold, cold ocean before they ever landed on our nice-place-ta-live.

(JUSTUS joins NELLIE in her light.)

JUSTUS. C'mon, Nellie.

NELLIE. Couldn't we just stay here a little longer, huh Jus? Oh, it's so peaceful here, so quiet.

JUSTUS. You will, Nellie. Pretty soon you'll be able to stay like this an nobody will take you from it. But right now, I need you to come back. C'mon, now.

(End of quiet. Lights back to all.)

I'll take his body towards to the water.

LULU. Gooch just said they're comin'.

JUSTUS. An he deserve to be put somewhere they won't ever get to him. Now I won't be gone far.

NELLIE. But…how long?

JUSTUS. I'm just headed to Gooch's spot.Not long.

NELLIE. But –

JUSTUS. Lu.

LULU. Don't worry, I wouldn't let Nellie to be left alone, Jus.

NELLIE. Hurry, Justus.

(JUSTUS exits, dragging GOOCH.)

Did you mean what ya said, Lu? 'Bout not leavin' me.

LULU. Of course, Nellie.

NELLIE. I don't think I could make it on my own.

LULU. I don't think you could either.

NELLIE. Well tha's not very a nice thing ta say.

LULU. You're not strong, Nellie. And you never will be.

NELLIE. What if I come with you though...?

LULU. Do you know what caught is, do you?

(NELLIE shakes her head.)

Caught is waking up every morning in a place you didn't ever choose or want to be. An you can't ever leave, you can't ever make choices again because they make them for you.

*(Lights shift to **JUSTUS** outside, he sits on the ground, looking soft. We should wonder why he's not hurrying back.)*

JUSTUS. ...I don't know what I'm doin' here, Rose Marie. I promised 'em I'd be back quick as I can. But lookit our spot, it's still here...

*(**JUSTUS** lays down, as though besides Rose Marie. Slowly, a large, looming shadow moves in over **JUSTUS**.)*

Don't you worry, Rosie, there's just a cloud passin' over that's all. The sun'll be back over you right quick.

*(**JUSTUS** gets up cautiously, looks up to shadow.)* I need you to git out of her sunlight. See you can have this whole everything, the bridge and river underneath it...but you cannot have this one spot. Cuz my Rose Marie is gonna come back to me, an this spot has to be here waitin' just how she remember it by.

*(**JUSTUS** crouches in an attacking position.)*

See you think I'm crazy. But me, even after all this, I can taste her in every breath I take in and I speak to her with every breath I send out. And I won't let any of your ugliness take that away.

*(The shadow moves in, **JUSTUS** grows horrifically with his teeth showing, readying to pounce. Lights shift back to **NELLIE** and **LULU**, they are standing frozen, listening to a loud, overbearing engine just outside. Sounds of tractoring over large constructs of wood and nature.*

*Just as the tractor seems to be shadowing over the room,
it pauses. The engine roars loudly before going idle.
Strange voices.)*

NELLIE. Can y'see 'em?

LULU. I think they're back behind the tractors. I...I can't
see what for though.

NELLIE. I don't wanna see 'em. What do they look like?

LULU. If I can see them, then they can see us, Nellie.

NELLIE. ...I thought they would talk like how we do.

LULU. Something's wrong.

NELLIE. But the engines stopped though.

LULU. If Jus is still out there, he's got no way of getting to
us."

NELLIE. But –

LULU. An if they wanted to tractor over us, they would
have.

NELLIE. What're you talkin' about, what're you even –

LULU. I need you to get yourself hid underneath those
blankets now, Nellie.

NELLIE. But –

LULU. Go on, Nellie! They are going to come in here and
if they see you –

NELLIE. I'm going, I'm going!

(**NELLIE** *begins hiding under blankets.)*

LULU. Now, Nellie, you do not move not even a movement
until...Do you understand.

NELLIE. ...I do...

(*Enter* **JUSTUS**, *he is with blood all over. His sisters
stare. They look sadly different from each other.)*

Jus!

LULU. What...what happened to you?

NELLIE. What's that covered all over you?

LULU. What happened?

NELLIE. Yer bleedin'!

JUSTUS. I'm not hurt, it's not me.

NELLIE. But there's blood.

LULU. Justus, lookit me. What happened?

JUSTUS. They're right outside.

NELLIE. Yer not cut, are ya?

LULU. Are you, are you hurt at all?

JUSTUS. Look, I'm not hurt, I'm fine –

NELLIE. But wait, what's the blood for, Jus, I don't understand.

JUSTUS. Please, Nellie.

LULU. It's all over you.

JUSTUS. Look, one day I will explain everything to you, but right now…Nellie, get to the back of the room. Get underneath them blankets an –

NELLIE. I know all about the blankets! Why're you bloody for, why're you –

LULU. Who's blood is that?

NELLIE. That's so much blood, it's too much.

LULU. Jus?

JUSTUS. Look, its not my blood, now Nellie, get yourself hid. Lu –

LULU. What did you do?

JUSTUS. Please.

LULU. …oh Justus please tell me you didn't –

NELLIE. Didn't what, what?

LULU. Is that what they stopped for, is that why they're outside like that?

NELLIE. Is what why, is what?

JUSTUS. Yes, Lu. They are lookin' for me an they won't stop until they –

NELLIE. Will somebody tell me what!

LULU. How could you!

JUSTUS. They put a bullet to somebody who did nothing with his life but love you. They captured an put a heap uh bodies filled with everyone we know an shared our lives with, every spot of everything we know is GONE… how could I not do –

LULU. They're waitin' on him, Nellie, because he killed one of 'em. They were waiting for him to get home. And now he is.

NELLIE. But they don't know. Justus he was quiet. They don't know him to be home.

LULU. I have to go.

NELLIE. Go where, Lu!

(*LULU moves towards exit.*)

LULU. I'm sorry.

JUSTUS. …don't leave yer family, Lu…don't do it…

LULU. I don't have a choice anymore!

NELLIE. They haven't come yet, they've stopped the tractorin', listen, I can't even hear 'em no more.

JUSTUS. You can choose to be with your family, Lu.

LULU. This is not being with your family, this is not that.

NELLIE. Yes, it is, here we are, we're right here.

LULU. Nellie, you remember, not a movement.

NELLIE. Please, Lulu…please. Justus, make her stay.

JUSTUS. Lu.

LULU. C'mon now, you two get down, I'm openin' up the door now.

NELLIE. No, don't let her go, Jus!

(*NELLIE jumps up towards LULU.*)

LULU & JUSTUS. Nellie!

(*Tractor engines rev up. JUSTUS grabs NELLIE.*)

NELLIE. …how can we just let go…how can we just let go what we call home?

(*LULU opens door, NELLIE surges, JUSTUS holds on.*)

JUSTUS. NELLIE.

(Just as LULU steps out, three large figures, standing twelve feet tall, with darkened, metallic masks covering their faces enter the room with animal-catching equipment. The moment they are in the space, NELLIE, LULU and JUSTUS drop to all fours. Dogs. The figures surround the family away from the door and pull nets.)

(LULU submits into a ball.)

(JUSTUS stands in front of NELLIE.)

(They loop LULU around the neck, throwing a net on her.)

(They pull a loop towards JUSTUS however he moves aggressively, growling, ready go pounce. A fourth twelve foot figure enters with a large baton and raises it to JUSTUS, who growls with vengeance in return. Lights out. End of Part I.)

PART II – THE INSIDE

"The cry of the poor is not always just, but if you don't listen to it, you will never know what justice is."

– Unknown

"If the world is saved, it will not be by old minds with new programs, but by new minds with no programs at all."

– Daniel Quinn

CHARACTERS

JUSTIN
ELEANOR
LUCY
GOON

Casting note: Same actors as in Part I

SETTING

Indoors

TIME

During progress

first scene

(Note: the characters in this part should attempt at a sort of Caucasian, almost upper class accent or way of speaking; despite the language. As the play goes on, this attempt should drop.)

(Lights up on a seemingly nice room. A spread is laid out, medium end fingerfoods and liquors. Glass glasses, silver-plated silverware.)

(Reveal **GOON**, *he looks a bit soiled, he picks at the food curiously and fixes himself a drink with a grin.)*

(Noise of fast footsteps and lauging coming from down the hall.)

(Bursts through the door **LUCY**, **JUSTIN**, *and* **ELEANOR**.)*

(They crash excitedly into to the table, ooh'ing and aah'ing as they knock over bottles and foods across the table.)

*(***GOON*** *backs up into the shadow, watching.)*

ELEANOR. Well thank God for the shit!

JUSTIN. Lookit that, Eleanor, I weren't even done with the last bottle uh this, an here I got me a fresh one right here.

ELEANOR. An see this here, Justin, got cheese in it. Lookit, I can't even grab onto it an it start leaking out, see.

*(***LUCY*** *downs a drink, makes another.)*

JUSTIN. Well thank you very much, Miss Lucy, for offerin' ta fix *our* drinks.

LUCY. I needed it.

JUSTIN. What, and we don't?

ELEANOR. I know I do. That what happened today just about fucked me up –

LUCY. What happened outside today was –

JUSTIN. What happened out there today was nothing. Ain't no reason to pay it anymore mind. Do you understand?

ELEANOR. Yea, Justin, I know, I got it.

LUCY. I just wish it we were done clearing already.

(JUSTIN *picks up a bottle.*)

JUSTIN. Aaight, I want this shit right here.

LUCY. What do you want mixed with it?

JUSTIN. How I know? I ain't ever had it before.

(JUSTIN *points out a few more bottles.*)

LUCY. Well do you want it just by itself then?

JUSTIN. How about some uh that right there, yea, put a little uh that in there with it.

ELEANOR. You know, while you waitin' on him, you coulda already poured me some uh that right there, two times, all way up.

JUSTIN. You in a hurry, Eleanor?

ELEANOR. Its free, ain't it? An if it free, I hurry.

(LUCY *passes drinks.*)

JUSTIN. *(to both)* Hey. You think there a real difference between the shit they stock us with, an the shit we drank back home? I mean do you think it really that much higher up? Or it's all just label.

ELEANOR. *(swirling her drink)* ...well it got the same basic taste. Shit smell the same too. *(She swallows.)* But...it go down a little easier, like I can't feel it hit my stomach as much, ya know? Makes me feel...higher-up.

LUCY. It's a higher quality.

JUSTIN. Wha'd I just say "higher-up" for? My amusements?

LUCY. Well, they're not just restocking for no reason.

JUSTIN. Can't you ever just enjoy life, Lu?

ELEANOR. Yea, why you gotta put so much thinking into free food and booze. It's free food and booze, all you gotta do is shut the fuck up.

JUSTIN. *(to* ELEANOR*)* Oh, that mouth uh yers is just about the dog in me. Go on, say that shit again.

ELEANOR. ...see, this is me, shutting the fuck up.

JUSTIN. You can't just leave a man hanging like that? C'mon, Eleanor, run that mouth a bit, just from here to here.

LUCY. Justin.

*(*JUSTIN *touches* ELEANOR *playfully, she plays along.)*

Ellie, you tell him to back off if you wish to.

(In the exchange, ELEANOR *spots* GOON*.)*

ELEANOR. Oh, shit!

JUSTIN. What're you gettin' all excited for, I ain't even done nothing worthwhile yet.

*(*ELEANOR *points out* GOON*, all look.)*

Well, what the fuck are you supposed to be?

LUCY. Is there something we can help you with? Are you here for –

JUSTIN. Speak, why don't ya.

GOON. 'M' called Goon.

JUSTIN. What?

ELEANOR. Was that...a language?

*(*GOON *reaches his hand out.)*

JUSTIN. Whoa, whoa, whoa, now you say your name is what?

ELEANOR. What kinda name's that? Goon. Sounds like maybe your parents didn't exactly feel like blessed when you showed up, huh?

LUCY. Is this your first day?

ELEANOR. First day?

LUCY. Ellie, shut up. *(pause)* Are you here because of today? Because of what happened out there –

JUSTIN. What can we help you with, Goon?

GOON. It is.

ELEANOR. What is.

GOON. My first day.

JUSTIN. You assigned here?

(**GOON** *nods.*)

LUCY. I'm Lucy, that's Eleanor, and yea, this is Justin.

GOON. Nice to meet you all.

ELEANOR. I don't know its exactly nice, but well, okay. Hi.

LUCY. We didn't mean to…whatever, we just didn't know they'd send us a replacement so soon –

JUSTIN. She just mean we don't know we necessarily need anybody new is all.

ELEANOR. So, is you custodial?

GOON. I was custodial, yes. But here I am, so I guess I must be moving up.

JUSTIN. They set you to clear?

GOON. I didn't really ask questions.

JUSTIN. So you could be custodial still.

LUCY. Justin, stoppit.

ELEANOR. You here to clean up after us, Goon, huh? You here to pick up what we don't feel like?

LUCY. Nevermind her, Goon.

GOON. I'm not here for custodial, I'm here to clear, just like you all.

LUCY. Are you hungry, do you need anything or –

JUSTIN. Lucy, why don't you freshen our drinks.

LUCY. I really don't feel like making drinks right now, Justin.

JUSTIN. Well that is your job.

LUCY. No, it's not actually. I just been doing it to be cordial.

JUSTIN. To be what?

LUCY. Cordial.

JUSTIN. What you usin' them big words for? Cordial. What that mean?

ELEANOR. Means nice.

JUSTIN. Then why didn't ya just say nice then?

ELEANOR. Maybe she tryin' to impress a certain… newcomer. Maybe she in love.

GOON. I certainly didn't mean to make such a fuss.

JUSTIN. See, now that's a good word. Fuss. It's simple. I can like see it, ya know. Fuss. Now, Lucy, instead of makin' such a fuss of things, why don't you just fix us some drinks. An if you wanna do it for bein' nice, go right on ahead.

(*LUCY makes drinks.*)

LUCY. Goon, would you like a refill?

JUSTIN. I asked first.

(**GOON** *nods,* **LUCY** *fixes. All watch as she hands* **GOON** *a drink.*)

GOON. Thank you.

LUCY. Ellie, what would you like?

ELEANOR. What you always askin' me what I'd like, Lucy, you know what I like.

(*LUCY fixes.*)

LUCY. Here ya are, two times.

ELEANOR. All the way up, oh yea, just the way I likes it.

LUCY. Justin?

(**JUSTIN** *walks over to her, up close, then places two bottles in front of her. She fixes from them.* **JUSTIN** *raises his glasses.*)

JUSTIN. To cordial.

GOON. Cordial.

LUCY. Cordial.

ELEANOR. Niceness.

(*They clink.*)

(a moment)

JUSTIN. So where were you assigned before then, Goon?

(**GOON** *finds his bearings, then points.*)

You see the way a conversation work, Goon, is that when I ask you a curiosity, you supposed to fill that curiosity. You don't just –

(**JUSTIN** *mocks pointing.*)

GOON. I have experience, if that's what you're asking about.

JUSTIN. No, it weren't. I asked where you was at.

(**GOON** *points with more authority.*)

You are one pointing motherfucker, ain't ya, Goon. Why I bet if you could, you'd just answer every fuckin' question with pointing, wouldn't you? "Hey, Goon, how you feelin' today?"

(**JUSTIN** *points down.*)

"So Goon, what'd you do today?"

(**JUSTIN** *points.*)

LUCY. Did they tell you why they were transferring you, Goon?

JUSTIN. What it matter why, Lucy, the man is here.

ELEANOR. What'd you mean you got experience, Goon, what'd that mean?

GOON. …

ELEANOR. Look, now he don't say nothin'.

JUSTIN. Yea, c'mon, Goon, you could at least *point.*

GOON. When I was custodial, I used to be in charge of cleaning out the containments.

ELEANOR. Ew, Goon, what would you wanna be in charge of that for.

GOON. I didn't choose to, Eleanor, anymore than you all chose this place.

ELEANOR. Ugh, that smell bein' so up' close all the time

with'em, don't that make your nose sad, Goon, don't it make sad your senses?

GOON. My nose still works. A little.

JUSTIN. So tell me, Goon, how do hosing out a buncha containments get you experience with clearing?

ELEANOR. His nose adapt, he can't smell no more, he perfect for getting right in there.

LUCY. What sort of experience were you referring to, Goon?

ELEANOR. Watch, I bet he answer when she ask, watch.

GOON. I spent a lot of time with them. Putting their food, cleaning up. Listening to them.

ELEANOR. Listening??? Wha's that mean, they don't talk, Goon.

GOON. Oh, but they do, Eleanor. All night they make sounds, I wondered even if they slept.

JUSTIN. Maybe you not clear on how languages work, Goon, but sounds ain't talking. See, if I do like this: (JUSTIN *burps.*) I ain't sayin' shit.

LUCY. What did you mean by listening, Goon?

ELEANOR. Oh, are we sure we wanna hear this, what if it give me the nightmares.

GOON. They scared me at first too, Eleanor. The pitches they would reach to. The guttural'ness of it all. I couldn't sleep not even an hour. But –

ELEANOR. What.

GOON. Pretty soon, I started noticing the patterns. Even noting down the positions of the moon. If it was wet outside or dry. Anything I could think of to just... make sense of them.

JUSTIN. That's an awful lot for custodial, ain't it?

GOON. That's where I was assigned to, Justin. That's where I spent my time. I would have had to completely go out of my way to ignore them if I didn't want to –

JUSTIN. What.

GOON. Wonder what they were saying.

ELEANOR. They just noise, Goon, what you mean saying? You think they was like, what, conversating an whatever, just like we do?

GOON. Not always, but sometimes.

(**ELEANOR** *laughs it up.*)

ELEANOR. Can't you just see this guy, bein' all like how he is, talkin' to 'em cuz he got nobody else to talk to.

LUCY. Shut up, Ellie.

JUSTIN. You talk to 'em, Goon, is that what you're here tellin'?

GOON. Yes. I do.

ELEANOR. Omigod, we got us a crazy up in here. Lucy, go on an hide all the sharp things wherever.

GOON. I don't mean we had discussions, Justin, but if you live alongside of something for long enough, you begin to...

LUCY. What were they saying?

JUSTIN. Yea, Goon, I'm awful curious myself, what have they said lately?

GOON. Just that they're scared; that they don't understand what it is we think we're doing.

ELEANOR. What they got to be scared for, they the ones got kept.

LUCY. That's really something, Goon, the way you look at things. Do you think you'll be able to...understand anything tomorrow?

ELEANOR. Omigod, wouldn't that just be like the thing, what if we was out there tomorrow and there be Goon all translatin 'an shit.

JUSTIN. Yea, Goon, you know now that I hear more about your...crazy talent, I do wish they had sent you along earlier tho'. Why we could've been listening to what they got to say this entire time we been here. Coulda used the entertainment. You think, Goon?

GOON. Think what?

JUSTIN. They entertainment?

GOON. Well my nights certainly have gotten more interesting since I learned to…

ELEANOR. Damn, Goon, what exactly do you mean by *entertainment*, what kinda *interesting nights* you talkin'?

LUCY. *(to* **ELEANOR***)* What the fuck is the matter with you?

ELEANOR. What, I ain't the one fuckin' some –

LUCY. Do you even have a thought running around inside that head of yours, Ellie?

ELEANOR. Yea, fact, I'm havin' one fuck of a thought right now. Keep talkin', we'll see how it develop.

*(***JUSTIN*** nudges* **GOON***.)*

JUSTIN. Hold onto yer drawers, Goon, we in for a little show.

LUCY. Yea, you do just have one thought only, don't you, Ellie, that's all your uneducated brain will allow, one at a time, little by little, you just let me know if ever we move too fast for you, you just go on and cut in.

ELEANOR. Goon, I want you to pay special good attention tonight, cuz you goin' hear a shitload uh sounds comin' outta Lucy's room all night. But I don't think you'll haffta translate them. They goin' be international as fuck.

LUCY. *(to* **GOON***)* There are those of us who are here and we work, Goon, and there are those of us who just fuckin' work here.

GOON. Well, I don't know which I am, but I am excited to get out there. Being cooped up inside that building for all this time, never seeing the daylight because I'm behind doors all day, I just…well, that is no way for a man to live. We are meant to be outside, I believe. Just like –

JUSTIN. Just like what?

GOON. Well, we were all born outside, we all –

ELEANOR. I weren't born outside, Goon, what the fuck you talkin'?

JUSTIN. Yea, was a hospital for me too, Goon. Sorry you had to go through that.

GOON. I just didn't like being assigned inside is all. I wasn't trying to –

LUCY. Trying to what?

GOON. I think I will bring something to the table tomorrow, that's all I'm saying actually. If absolutely nothing else, I will be excited to finally be outside with –

JUSTIN. With?

GOON. You all. And them. All of us.

JUSTIN. Us?

LUCY. Justin.

JUSTIN. You know, if you want, I can let you keep one of 'em tomorrow Goon. That way you can go on with your communications an all. You know, so you don't miss out on any entertainment.

ELEANOR. Shut up, Jus. Tha's the stupidest thing I ever heard.

LUCY. Don't listen to him, Goon, he don't even have close the authority to –

JUSTIN. I'm the one doin' it, I got the authority to do whatever it is I want.

LUCY. No ya don't, Jus, *they* tell us what.

ELEANOR. Es true, they tell us the shit.

JUSTIN. *I'm* the one on the front lines, *I'm* the one doin' the work, don't you tell me I got no say, Ellie.

ELEANOR. You got no say, Jus.

JUSTIN. Goon, what do you say? Would you like to take one for yourself tomorrow?

LUCY. Don't listen to him, he's fulla shit.

ELEANOR. Goon, in all my time, I never seen him not do what he say.

LUCY. Do *you* believe him, Ellie?

ELEANOR. No, but tha's just cuz I know him.

JUSTIN. Goon?

GOON. That's really not necessary, Justin. Thank you for the offer though.

JUSTIN. Awh, come on now, you tellin' me you don't want me to just keep one for your amusements?

GOON. No. I don't.

JUSTIN. Fine. Still a good idea tho'.

GOON. I think I'll be plenty entertained just by being out there, Justin. I'm even kinda nervous, bout what its like.

LUCY. I don't know that you'll like it, Goon. It's ugly.

ELEANOR. It ain't all ugly.

LUCY. Mostly it is, Ellie.

ELEANOR. It can be funny tho, Goon. Out there. Sometimes we get to laughin'. Yea, right in the middle the work day, we laughin' like we was on our own time. Oh, can I just let him something funny from today, Jus, just one little thing?

LUCY. Eleanor, just let it.

ELEANOR. When I'm bout to do something I ain't ever done before, I like to get as much information as is possible. So even if this particular funny isn't your type of funny, least you'll be that much more knowing.

GOON. Go on.

ELEANOR. So…we're over by this heap an – wait, you prolly don't know what's a heap, do you.

GOON. I do.

ELEANOR. You do? How do you know what a heap is, is that like a thing? Me, I thought it was just our own little whatever. Well, not maybe *little*, cuz between you an me, Goon, its kinda gotten big. *(pause)* Oh, you prolly seen it tho', huh?

GOON. No, but I've heard.

ELEANOR. Okay, so we're by the heap this morning about to pile more shit on top, well it wasn't actually shit, Goon, that's not what we do with our shit –

GOON. I get it.

ELEANOR. Well, just in case you don't know we got plumbing. We got plumbing regular.

SO, just as we get to the heap, we see...

(*She begins laughing,* **JUSTIN** *giggles.*)

...well we see these movements. But not like, well... sometimes when yer heapin' things, they not always dead, ya know. Sometimes they still got the nerves movin'.

But well, this wasn't nerves.

See there was two of *them*. Jus' standin' on the side of that heap an they's doin' like this funny holdin' on, ya know. Almost looked like they was pro'creatin. An my my did they stink. You could almost see their stink, all around 'em. Like in that cartoon, you know?

So when they heard us comin', they thrown themselves on the side of the heap an jus' played like dead.

So know what we do? We buried one of 'em.

Yea, the one in front, the one bein' held onto from behind. We heaped all our shit from the morning right on top of it. Just to see if it could make its way out from under.

You ever do that?

Growin 'up. We'd be playin' around the house, an I'd pour all these blankets on top uh our dog, see how long it take for it to figure it all out.

Or how bout like with a baby? Put a blanket over it, just to see if she'll push the blanket away or if you gotta do it for her.

GOON. Did she make it out?

ELEANOR. Who, the baby? Nah, tha's just an example of my story, Goon.

GOON. Today. At the heap.

ELEANOR. Oh, I don't think so. I waited around to see if I
saw any movements, you know, of it getting out from
under. But it was still as stillness can be. I thought it'd
be so cute if it crawled itself out. But nah, probably it
couldn't figure it out. Needed me to help it. Just like a
dog. Or that imaginary baby.

JUSTIN. In this place, you got to know the differences
between things, Goon.

Cuz the better you learn that *them* and *us* ain't even
the same…atmosphere, the better you're gonna be at
this life.

A man got to know where he stand with things. What
goes where an who belongs to who.

(**JUSTIN** *clinks* **GOON***'s glass, downs his drink then
throws his glass to the floor; it shatters.*)

LUCY. What is the matter with you?

ELEANOR. We're gonna get the shards all over our feet.

JUSTIN. Drink up, Goon.

LUCY. Custodial don't come till tomorrow, Jus.

ELEANOR. What if I wanted to sneak out for some eats if I
can't sleep tonight. I won't know where to step.

(**LUCY** *and* **ELEANOR** *begin picking up shards.* **GOON**
downs his drink, **JUSTIN** *urges him to throw his glass,
he refuses.*)

JUSTIN. Leave it be, ladies.

LUCY. Oh, so you'll clean it then?

ELEANOR. An we all know its goin *me* that winds up with
cut feet.

JUSTIN. So don't step then.

LUCY. Its gonna stain the floor, its gonna get all sticky.

JUSTIN. C'mon, Luce, say that again. Sticky sound good
comin' outta you.

ELEANOR. We ought take all this spilt glass an circle it
around Justin's bed, that's what we ought do.

JUSTIN. Y'hear that, Goon? That is some sweet music, ain't it?

LUCY. No, Ellie, nevermind him, don't even give him the notice.

(**LUCY** and **ELEANOR** *bent over on their hands and knees, cleaning. They freeze.* **JUSTIN** *begins to encircle them, as though they are his prey.*)

JUSTIN. So…?

GOON. So?

JUSTIN. Which would you?

GOON. Which would I what?

(**JUSTIN** *walks over towards* **ELEANOR**, *nudging her sexually from behind with his foot.*)

JUSTIN. If I could stop time, Goon, an just…do whatever the fuck, well this is the one I'd go to. Ooh, yea, got a nice little shape, got a good scent, hell I think I can scent her from here. An lookit her circumference, just my size, ya know. Ooh yea.

An how 'bout you then?

(*A moment before* **GOON** *reluctantly acknowledges* **LUCY**.)

That one, huh? Yea, that one's got nice parts to boot. Not necessarily my exact sort, but who we kiddin', huh Goon, either piece'd do, huh! Ha, look at 'em. On the floor like that, just…perfectly placed…

(**JUSTIN** *circles the women, nudging different with his feet.*)

Know what I'd like, hell I could even do it with her on the floor bent over like so. I'd peel this off like that. Pull them down all the way right there. An guess where I'd put myself in. Go on, you ain't ever goin' guess.

GOON. …

JUSTIN. I'd put it right in that little spot right there. Know how come?

GOON. I don't.

JUSTIN. Cuz sometimes we gotta create our own holes, Goon. *(pause)* Now you go.

GOON. Oh, well it has been awhile since I even come up close to a...I don't know I'd even be able to –

JUSTIN. Go.

GOON. Well, I guess, if I could...stop the time, like you said, I'd probably just wanna be right in there.

JUSTIN. Whoa, whoa, whoa, you can't just rush to the end like that. You gotta paint me through it. Now go on, take 'er slow.

GOON. ...okay. I guess –

JUSTIN. Not you guess, yer a man, tell me what you know.

GOON. ...I'd want to –

JUSTIN. Not you'd want. Say it like you don't have to want nothin', it's yours.

GOON. I'd pull this back, so its out of the way. An I would glide these down right about there. An I'd wrap myself around, just right there.

JUSTIN. An the hole? *(**GOON** points.)*

GOON. That one right there.

JUSTIN. See that, Goon.

GOON. No.

JUSTIN. See, even in a four-person room, you an me, we're more the same than even they.

*(**JUSTIN** takes **GOON**'s hand, smacks it with bravado. They freeze like that. Meanwhile **LUCY** an **ELEANOR** unfreeze.)*

ELEANOR. Hey, Lu.

LUCY. What is it, Ellie?

ELEANOR. Do you ever get scared to go back outside? I mean after what happened today, I mean what another one of them things go crazy on us?

LUCY. What do you let him get his paws on you for, Ellie?

ELEANOR. Wuz that my question?

LUCY. I'm trying to answer your question, Ellie. Why do you.

ELEANOR. Well, he goin' do what he do anyways, I'm just keepin' on his good side is all. Geez, what'd you think, I's lettin' him for?

LUCY. If you don't like something, then don't do it.

ELEANOR. I do *not* think you are answering my question. I think yer sittin' there on your hands and knees and judgin' me like yer not doin' things *you* don't wanna do.

LUCY. You're right.

ELEANOR. No shit.

LUCY. But don't you ever wonder who it really is going crazy out there?

ELEANOR. So do you then, get scared to go back out?

LUCY. I'm scared right now, Ellie, I'm perfectly fucking frightened.

(*A tableau of the women on the floor and cleaning, men shaking hands above them. Lights down.*)

last scene

(Lights up on the same room, restocked.)

(Enter **ELEANOR**, *she opens a bottle and puts back.)*

(Enter **LUCY**, *she open her own bottle, takes it to the face.)*

(Enter **GOON** *with blood up his arms.)*

(Both stare at him as he takes a bottle with his head back.)

(The thumping of a man's workboots are heard.)

(Enter **JUSTIN**, *he looks like he got his ass kicked.)*

(He puts his own bottle to his mouth.)

JUSTIN. *(to* **GOON***)* You.

GOON. …

JUSTIN. I said, You.

GOON. And I heard you.

JUSTIN. I want you, to explain to me, just what in the fuck.

GOON. …I might've…got carried away.

ELEANOR. *That* was carried away?

LUCY. Goon, why don't I fix you a drink.

JUSTIN. Our job was to clear the area, not…

ELEANOR. You scared the living everything right out from inside me.

LUCY. From all of us.

GOON. Good.

JUSTIN. Of course we were scared, there was a fuckin' savage with us.

LUCY. Please, Goon, have a glass, have some ice; cool down a bit, huh.

(She fixes.)

JUSTIN. *(to* **GOON***)* So?

GOON. So what?

JUSTIN. Amuse me.

LUCY. Here.

JUSTIN. Lucy –

(**GOON** *takes drink, drinks.*)

Fine. Now, talk.

ELEANOR. Yea, what was the matter in your head that you'd –

I can't even mouth it.

JUSTIN. Try massacre.

GOON. I apologize if I frightened you all.

LUCY. I don't understand, Goon, I just –

ELEANOR. What the hell would you do that for?!

JUSTIN. I got you now, Goon, I known there was something, I couldn't put my finger on it, but…you a crazy. That why they reassign you? Talkin' to what don't talk back. Lookin' like how you do. You a nutjob motherfucker an here we are in the same room wit' you.

LUCY. Why don't you just take awhile, Goon. Sit. Just try to –

Nobody thinks you're crazy.

ELEANOR. That was the bloodiest thing I ever seen with my eyes, so if that ain't crazed, I…I can't even think straight, I wish I hadn't seen that. I wish I hadn't gone back out there.

LUCY. Was it too much for you, being outside again after so long –

ELEANOR. I didn't know they could scream like that. Goon, I never heard a pitch go up that high.

LUCY. Maybe you're sick, Goon, maybe –

GOON. Lookit me. It almost looks like *I* got hurt in all this, don't it? Lookit all this blood.

ELEANOR. *Did* you get hurt?

GOON. No, this is all theirs; it's just same color as ours.

LUCY. Maybe you've been out here too long, maybe, I don't know, maybe –

JUSTIN. Yea, what're you so fucked up for, Goon?

GOON. I see what ya meant about the nerves, Eleanor. The way they shudder.

ELEANOR. Justin right, you a crazy fuck, ain't ya.

GOON. I don't see what I done out there is any more crazy than that heap.

ELEANOR. We was okay to 'em, Goon, we put 'em a shot so they don't go nowhere, but then we…

GOON. What, Ellie, then you what?

LUCY. We would bleed them by their throat.

ELEANOR. Well, yea, when you put it like that, Lucy, it don't sound so nice, but –

GOON. It's okay, Eleanor, you can talk to me about the heap now, I get it. About heaping things on top, I understand. About that imaginary baby, yea, I can picture it now. *(pause)* See, you all call me crazy, but…I don't think I'm anymore far gone than you all.

LUCY. It's not Ellie's fault. She's just –

GOON. Just what?

LUCY. She's just doin', has been doing, what she's paid to do.

ELEANOR. …I didn't…I didn't know it that way, I didn't know they…

LUCY. It's okay, Ellie.

JUSTIN. Go on, grab yourself a two-times all the way up, Ellie. Go on now.

(ELEANOR gets drinks.)

GOON. I know.

JUSTIN. You know what?

GOON. I know you didn't know. *(pause)* Eleanor, you okay?

LUCY. She's fine.

ELEANOR. No, I ain't. I ain't fine. I ain't fine with this no more.

JUSTIN. Just calm yerself, Eleanor, now we don't have anything else to clear, pretty soon we'll have us new tasks to put, an there won't be none of this to even remember. Why pretty soon, this'll all settle, an we'll have homes put, little ones runnin' around –

LUCY. Don't lie to her, Justin. You have absolutely no idea what happens next.

JUSTIN. What have we been doin' here, Lucy, if not making it safe for us to start our homes, begin our families.

LUCY. It's not up to you, Justin. What we do. We'll do whatever work it is they want worked. And it might be scary. It might be every bit as ugly –

JUSTIN. Lucy, cut it. Ellie don't need to hear that right now.

ELEANOR. No, what I need is to get up outta here.

GOON. Eleanor might have a point, you know.

JUSTIN. Goon, shut up.

GOON. Imagine what the outside think of us now.

ELEANOR. An just what is that supposed ta mean, Goon?

JUSTIN. Ellie, don't you listen to him, there isn't anything left out there. We done cleared the area, fact, nutjob motherfucker here cleared the living shit out of it.

GOOCH. Oh, we've cleared the settlements, sure, Justin. But you and I know there is a lot more out in that world than just what we been clearing. There are thousands of eyes still out there watchin'. Thousands of every size, of every shape. There are so many thousands of different sorts all staring at every move we make now. All of 'em scared. And we are the enemy to every single one of them.

JUSTIN. Well, that's just fuckin' great, Goon. So they'll prolly stay hid, won't they? Maybe crawl into our Earth. Breeding under where we walk. Populating our dirt.

Why they'll be so many of them down there scared to come out, they'll make the ground earthquake when they move.

And that's how we'll go on living. Trying to raise our own famlilies right on top of theirs. Walkin' around every day tryin' to be happy, but just below, right underneath, why there's entire civilizations, of God only knows, wishin' us dead.

ELEANOR. So what, we're just supposed to keep on tryin' to be here, huh? I can't do that, Justin, I can't get used to a life like this.

JUSTIN. No, we'll clear them, Ellie. Every single pocket, every single cluster. One thousand, two, it don't matter. We'll find them cuz we are not meant to be scared 'for, Ellie. Livin' on the surface of things? Us up here an them down there?

No, nuh-uh, there is a whole world out there, an I'll be damned if I'm goin' tell my children they ought be scared to be a part of it.

LUCY. What do we tell our children then, Justin? Huh? That this is all okay? "Here you are, go an play, an don't you worry about nothing, your mommy and daddy have already murdered everything out the way. So go on. Cuz the entire world is just so beautiful."

ELEANOR. No, nuh uh I don't want children uh mine anywhere near ugliness like this.

LUCY. Neither do I.

ELEANOR. What if they don't wanna be in a place like this, what if they don't wanna...be on top of things...what if they don't wanna...

LUCY. We can leave, Ellie.

JUSTIN. Now look, I am not going to be made to pay the sins for this lone, nutjob motherfucker. One man do not all of us make.

ELEANOR. I'm goin' tell them. I'm goin' say it that I quit. I can't be here no more. I just wanna go home.

JUSTIN. Look, we have us a roof over our heads, we have us food better than my mouth ever come across, an top shelf shit down our throats.

LUCY. How long do you think they are going to keep re-stocking things for us, Jus?

JUSTIN. Until we feel comfortable bein' here!

ELEANOR. Oh, I won't ever be comfortable here, nuh uh, not me.

LUCY. I knew it, Jus, I knew you was scared.

JUSTIN. 'M' not scared.

LUCY. That what all this was for, Justin, don't you see. This room, that spread, everything was for us to just…be okay with everything. That we wouldn't notice as the days turned to years. And the years to generations. We are a living distraction, Justin. And I don't feel like being distracted no more.

JUSTIN. This is our job, Lucy. This is how we do our part.

LUCY. Part of what, Jus?

JUSTIN. This is how it work, if we need to expand out this way, then they need people to clear the area. What is so goddamned complicated about that, huh? An so what if we the ones that do it. Least I got to saving for my children.

LUCY. You say we're expanding? Who is? Us? I dunno about you, Jus, but this is about the same day-in-day-out work that I done back home. My life hasn't expanded one bit. And I' not bein' paid extra to –

ELEANOR. Bleed things by they throat.

JUSTIN. We aren't animals, we do things for the greater good. We do things not just for us, but for our –

LUCY. Children, yea, I got that. What about them?

JUSTIN. The more we grow, the more we have, as a…as a people. The more we have, the more our children will –

LUCY. We will never have what you're daydreaming, Justin. We will never work enough to have more than what we got right here. Our lives, they are fixed. You think you in charge of the clearing? You're not. You're just doing the labor. Nothing more.

ELEANOR. You know, I thought the food an booze was gonna be all the time forever.

LUCY. It's not.

ELEANOR. But d'you know something? Did you ever notice, this room. It's really not that nice. The other night, well, I was drunk as skunks, so I started messin' about with that shit over there, an that over there. Cuz that's how I do. An you know, they just covered up shit stuff with nice stuff. It ain't really nice underneath. Fact, look to me like a junk space. Where they keep for leftovers. An I didn't wanna say nothin' cuz we seemed to be havin' such a time here, but when I saw that, I kinda felt like leftovers too.

*(**ALL** look at each other. A light shift, they all move with it. Lower submissive. Appears **GOOCH**, he looks around like foreign. A moment. Appears **LULU** and **JUSTUS**.)*

GOOCH. I led them to you, Lulu, I'm sorry.

JUSTUS. Wasn't you that brought them to us, Gooch.

*(**GOOCH** confuses.)*

I got my temper up an you know how that go

LULU. Things turned out okay, though, Gooch. For me and Justus; Nellie.

GOOCH. Really? Cuz you two look like shit.

JUSTUS. They went a little crazy on us, Gooch. They slit a lot more than our throats when we went.

GOOCH. I'm sorry, Lu.

JUSTUS. What, just her? Ain't you sorry for me?

GOOCH. I am, but just imagining my Lu all –

JUSTUS. Know what's funny.

LULU. What's that?

JUSTUS. Just as they was comin'at me the words with their devices, I almost wished it.

GOOCH. Wished what?

JUSTUS. For them to just get on with it. To just...let it out on us, all how angry they seem to be, all how lonely they seem to be, all of it, just let it all out on me an Lu cuz –

LULU. Know what's funnier than that? I was thinking the same thing. I was thinking they should just let everything out cuz –

JUSTUS. Cuz Nellie?

LULU. Cuz Nellie.

GOOCH. I was afraid to ask.

JUSTUS. They didn't get to her, Gooch. They never even laid eyes.

LULU. They were so entertained by me an Jus, yea, she just stayed there an –

(appears **NELLIE***)*

JUSTUS. Oh, no. Nellie, what're you…what're you doin' here?

NELLIE. Oh, don't worry, ya'll, I don't think I'm really here. I mean, not like ya'll. I don't get massacred or anything like that if that's what you're wondering.

LULU. But –

NELLIE. Nothing will happen to me for quite some time, Lu. Thank you for that.

JUSTUS. You look perfect, Nellie, you look just like…

NELLIE. You remember me by?

JUSTUS. Remember you by?

NELLIE. That's the way you always put it, ain't it Jus. Guess I picked stuff up from you all the time an didn't even know it.

GOOCH. You okay tho', Nellie-belly?

NELLIE. Things are…nice, Gooch, since my entire family got murdered. Different, but okay, I guess.

JUSTUS. You hurt or –

NELLIE. No, I ain't hurt.

LULU. You look safe.

NELLIE. Well, I am maybe.

LULU. That's all that matters then.

NELLIE. Is it?

LULU. What d'you mean?

NELLIE. Oh, I don't know how to explain things, Lu. Just… my belly is happy. An everything is warm all the time, but –

JUSTUS. What.

NELLIE. I used to *feel* things. I used to feel so many things. For you Jus, Lu an Gooch. But now, just everything goes on an on like one long daytime day. An I can't tell one part from the next cuz it's all just so nice. *(pause)* An I know sometimes y'all used to scare the Nellie outta me. But, least I could hear my heart inside. Least I could smell when you Jus and you Lu was worried for me, least I could feel the ground when I know something wasn't right. Oh an I used to love eating how we ate. Was like I got to use all my senses. Right, Jus?

JUSTUS. Right.

NELLIE. An now…

JUSTUS. I'm sorry I –

LULU. We should've –

NELLIE. Oh, enough with that. Could be worse. *(pause)* I should go.

LULU. Where, how come?

(NELLIE shrugs.)

NELLIE. …just cuz.

GOOCH. Can't you stay?

JUSTUS. Just a little while more, Nellie.

NELLIE. Can I ask just one thing tho'?

LULU. Anything.

NELLIE. How long do I haffta stay here?

(Lights back to people.)

LUCY. We're not stayin' here, Justin. I am through working here.

JUSTIN. So what then?

ELEANOR. We go, we quit..

JUSTIN. What do you think happens if we jump ship, huh? You think work will be waitin' for us back home? You think anybody goin' hire us like that?

No, we got to stay here. And work. I don't see what we got any choice but that.

GOON. I heard pretty soon they goin' have us put a concrete ground outside. That'll keep everyone safe from anything underneath, won't it? I heard they also goin' have us put blinking alert lights, and more buildings built so high that they'll crowd the sky. And we won't have anything to worry about maybe. And the days will be nice, maybe.

JUSTIN. …yea nice…see that, he got a crazy-ass way uh puttin' it, but we goin' be alright here, Ellie, Lucy.

LUCY. No, we're not.

ELEANOR. Let they do they own clearin', killin', an whatever other ugly things they need for. Fuck 'em

LUCY. Fuck 'em.

(Sounds from outside the room. Intense. All look around scared.)

JUSTIN. You two shut your goddamned mouths. What the hell are you doin' talking like that so loud for, huh?

ELEANOR. Who out there, Jus?

LUCY. It's them.

ELEANOR. I know it's a them, but which one, I can't keep track.

GOON. I just hope –

ELEANOR. Hope what?

GOON. I just hope its people.

ELEANOR. Well, what the hell does that mean, Goon.

GOON. People we can talk to. But…

LUCY. What.

GOON. If those thousands of different-sized eyes have all…

ELEANOR. What, what, say it, you tryin' to put a quake in my heart, geez!

GOON. If they got all those different sorts, all them different species got together, like all together, like thousands upon thousands all at once, and are…

JUSTIN. What, and are what?

GOON. Going to try an get in here.

JUSTIN. They can't get in, we got doors, we got locks locked.

GOON. What do you think locks an doors will do to numbers like their numbers?

JUSTIN. Look, everybody calm. If it…if it ain't people, if it is…like Goon say, we got nothing to worry about, we got a whole settlement of people here to help us.

ELEANOR. Yea, but they gonna help us now, after how we talked 'bout leavin'?

LUCY. We don't have thousands, Justin. Not even close.

JUSTIN. Look, are smarter than them, we –

GOON. It won't matter, they outnumber us. If it is them all gathered up into one…stampede, we only have a few moments left.

ELEANOR. We could apologize or some shit. We could tell them how it wasn't us. How we're just the workers, we're just the –

LUCY. They won't understand that, Ellie.

ELEANOR. Goon can tell 'em, he can talk.

LUCY. That won't make one difference, Eleanor.

JUSTIN. Well why the fuck not?!

LUCY. Because, we all look the same to them.

(Sounds grow. They seem to be coming from in every direction. A jarring thud hits the doors in the room; all close in close to each other, grabbing hold of each other without notice. The doors of the space burst open. Lights blacken fast. Curtain. End of play.)